My Calm-Down Books

I CAN TALK

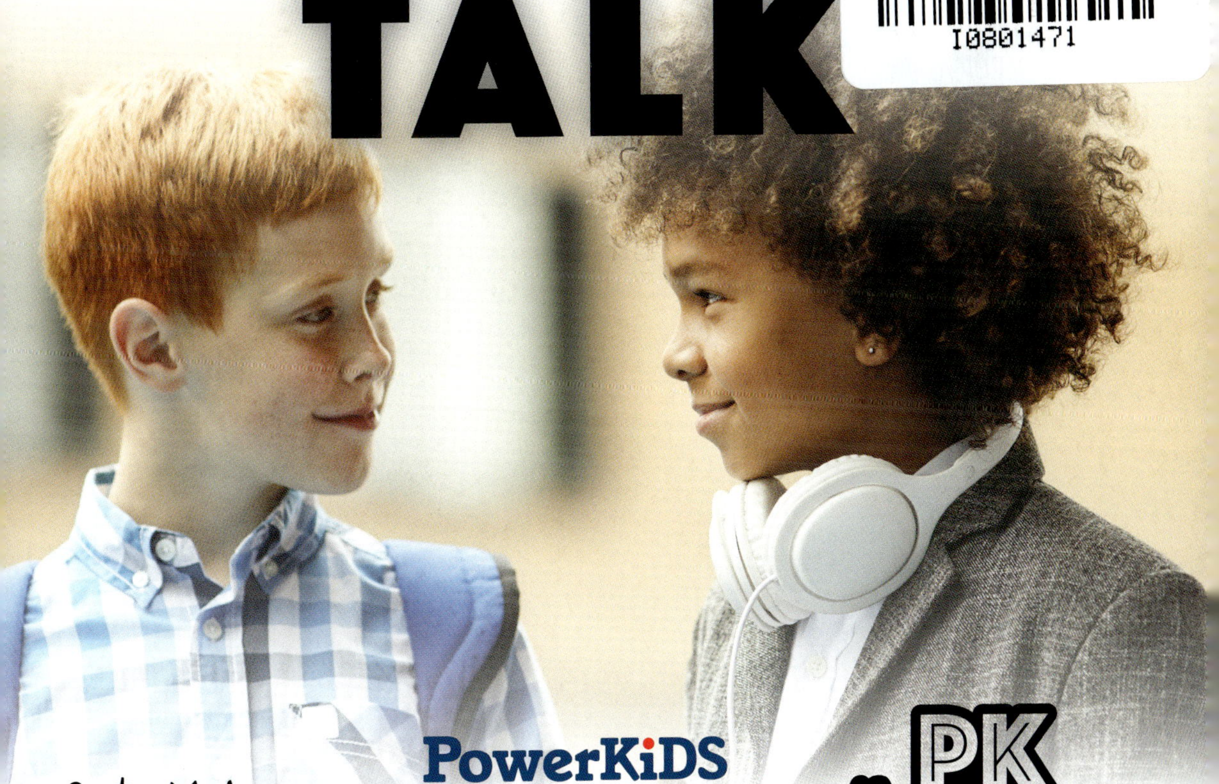

Caitie McAneney

PowerKiDS press

PK Beginners

I have lots of feelings. Sometimes they feel too big.

Sometimes I feel scared.

I want to hide.

Sometimes I feel
sad or mad.
I want to cry or yell.

I feel alone.
Will other people
understand how I feel?

I talk to my parents.
They care about me.

I talk to my friends.
They understand.

I talk to my teacher.
She helps me.

I talk to a counselor. She says big feelings are okay!

I talk to people I trust. I tell them my fears and feelings.

Some people
just listen.
Some people help.

I let it all out.

I feel much better!

Published in 2024 by The Rosen Publishing Group, Inc.
2544 Clinton Street, Buffalo, NY 14224

First Edition

Editor: Caitie McAneney
Book Design: Rachel Rising

Photo Credits: Cover, p. 1 AnnaStills/Shutterstock.com; p. 3 Rawpixel.com/Shutterstock.com; p. 5 Asier Romero/Shutterstock.com; pp. 7, 17 Prostock-studio/Shutterstock.com; p. 9 Veja/Shutterstock.com; p. 11 Ground Picture/Shutterstock.com; pp. 13, 21 Monkey Business Images/Shutterstock.com; p. 15 michaeljung/Shutterstock.com; p. 19 wavebreakmedia/Shutterstock.com; p. 23 New Africa/Shutterstock.com.

Cataloging-in-Publication Data
Names: McAneney, Caitie.
Title: I can talk / Caitie McAneney.
Description: New York : Powerkids Press, 2024. | Series: My calm-down books
Identifiers: ISBN 9781642825008 (pbk.) | ISBN 9781642825015 (library bound) | ISBN 9781642825022 (ebook)
Subjects: LCSH: Interpersonal communication in children--Juvenile literature.
Classification: LCC BF723.C57 M45 2024 | DDC 155.4'136--dc23

Manufactured in the United States of America

CPSIA Compliance Information: Batch #CSPK24 For further information contact Rosen Publishing at 1-800-237-9932.